THE THIRD PERSON

BY

HENRY JAMES

British Library Cataloguing-in-Publication Data
A catalogue record for this book is available from
the British Library

Contents

HENRY JAMES

Henry James was born in New York City in 1843. One of thirteen children, James had an unorthodox early education, switching between schools, private tutors and private reading. In 1855, the James family embarked on a three year-long trip to Geneva, London, and Paris; an experience that greatly influenced his decision, some years later, to emigrate to Europe. Having returned to America, and having met prominent authors and thinkers such as Ralph Waldo Emerson and Henry David Thoreau, James turned seriously to writing.

James published his first story, 'A Tragedy of Error', in the *Continental Monthly* in 1864, when he was twenty years old. In 1876, he emigrated to London, where he remained for the vast majority of the rest of his life, becoming a British citizen in 1915. From this point on, he was a hugely prolific author, eventually producing twenty novels and more than a hundred short stories and novellas, as well as literary criticism, plays and travelogues.

Amongst James's most famous works are *The Europeans* (1878), *Daisy Miller* (1878), *Washington Square* (1880), *The Bostonians* (1886), and one of the most famous ghost stories of all time, *The Turn of the Screw* (1898). James' personal favourite, of all his works, was the 1903 novel *The Ambassadors*. He is regarded by modern-day critics as one of the key figures of 19th-century literary realism, and one of the greatest American authors of all-time.

James' autobiography appeared in three volumes between 1914 and 1917. He died following a stroke in February of 1916, aged 72.

THE THIRD PERSON

Henry James

I

When, a few years since, two good ladies, previously not intimate nor indeed more than slightly acquainted, found themselves domiciled together in the small but ancient town of Marr, it was as a result, naturally, of special considerations. They bore the same name and were second cousins; but their paths had not hitherto crossed; there had not been coincidence of age to draw them together; and Miss Frush, the more mature, had spent much of her life abroad. She was a bland, shy, sketching person, whom fate had condemned to a monotony – triumphing over variety – of Swiss and Italian *pensions*; in any one of which, with her well-fastened hat, her gauntlets and her stout boots, her camp-stool, her sketch-book, her Tauchnitz novel, she would have served with peculiar propriety as a frontispiece to the natural history of the English old maid. She would have struck you indeed, poor Miss Frush, as so happy an instance of the type that you would perhaps scarce have been able to equip her with the dignity of the individual. This was what she enjoyed, however, for those brought nearer –

a very insistent identity, once even of prettiness, but which now, blanched and bony, timid and inordinately queer, with its utterance all vague interjection and its aspect all eyeglass and teeth, might be acknowledged without inconvenience and deplored without reserve. Miss Amy, her kinswoman, who, ten years her junior, showed a different figure – such as, oddly enough, though formed almost wholly in English air, might have appeared much more to betray a foreign influence – Miss Amy was brown, brisk, and expressive: when really young she had even been pronounced showy. She had an innocent vanity on the subject of her foot, a member which she somehow regarded as a guarantee of her wit, or at least of her good taste. Even had it not been pretty she flattered herself it would have been shod: she would never – no, never, like Susan – have given it up. Her bright brown eye was comparatively bold, and she had accepted Susan once for all as a frump. She even thought her, and silently deplored her as, a goose. But she was none the less herself a lamb.

They had benefited, this innocuous pair, under the will of an old aunt, a prodigiously ancient gentlewoman, of whom, in her later time, it had been given them, mainly by the office of others, to see almost nothing; so that the little property they came in for had the happy effect of a windfall. Each, at least, pretended to the other that she had never dreamed – as in truth there had been small encouragement for dreams in the sad character of what they now spoke of as the late lady's "dreadful *entourage*." Terrorized and deceived, as they considered, by her own people, Mrs Frush was scantily enough to have been counted on for an act of almost inspired justice. The good luck of her husband's nieces was that she had really outlived, for the most part, their ill-wishers and so, at the very last, had died without the blame of diverting fine Frush property from fine Frush use. Property quite of her own she had done as she liked with; but she had pitied poor expatriated Susan and had remembered poor unhusbanded Amy, though lumping them together perhaps a little roughly in her final provision.

Her will directed that, should no other arrangement be more convenient to her executors, the old house at Marr might be sold for their joint advantage. What befell, however, in the event, was that the two legatees, advised in due course, took an early occasion – and quite without concert – to judge their prospects on the spot. They arrived at Marr, each on her own side, and they were so pleased with Marr that they remained. So it was that they met: Miss Amy, accompanied by the office-boy of the local solicitor, presented herself at the door of the house to ask admittance of the caretaker. But when the door opened it offered to sight not the caretaker, but an unexpected, unexpecting lady in a very old waterproof, who held a long-handled eyeglass very much as a child holds a rattle. Miss Susan, already in the field, roaming, prying, meditating in the absence on an errand of the woman in charge, offered herself in this manner as in settled possession; and it was on that idea that, through the eyeglass, the cousins viewed each other with some penetration even before Amy came in. Then at last when Amy did come in it was not, any more than Susan, to go out again.

It would take us too far to imagine what might have happened had Mrs Frush made it a condition of her benevolence that the subjects of it should inhabit, should live at peace together, under the roof she left them; but certain it is that as they stood there they had at the same moment the same unprompted thought. Each became aware on the spot that the dear old house itself was exactly what she, and exactly what the other, wanted; it met in perfection their longing for a quiet harbour and an assured future; each, in short, was willing to take the other in order to get the house. It was therefore not sold; it was made, instead, their own, as it stood, with the dead lady's extremely "good" old appurtenances not only undisturbed and undivided, but piously reconstructed and infinitely admired, the agents of her testamentary purpose rejoicing meanwhile to see the business so simplified. They might have had their private doubts – or their wives might have; might cynically have predicted the sharpest of quarrels, before three months were out, between the deluded yoke-fellows, and the dissolution of the partnership with every circumstance of recrimination. All that need be said is that such prophets would have prophesied vulgarly. The Misses Frush were not vulgar; they had drunk deep of the cup of singleness and found it prevailingly bitter; they were not unacquainted with solitude and sadness, and they recognized with due humility the supreme opportunity of their lives. By the end of three months, moreover, each knew the worst about the other. Miss Amy took her evening nap before dinner, an hour at which Miss Susan could never sleep – it was so odd; whereby Miss Susan took hers after that meal, just at the hour when Miss Amy was keenest for talk. Miss Susan, erect and unsupported, had feelings as to the way in which, in almost any posture that could pass for a seated one, Miss Amy managed to find a place in the small of her back for two out of the three sofa-cushions – a smaller place, obviously, than they had ever been intended to fit.

But when this was said all was said; they continued to have, on either side, the pleasant consciousness of a personal soil, not devoid of fragmentary ruins, to dig in. They had a theory that their lives had been immensely different, and each appeared now to the other to have conducted her career so perversely only that she should have an unfamiliar range of anecdote for her companion's ear. Miss Susan, at foreign *pensions*, had met the Russian, the Polish, the Danish, and even an occasional flower of the English, nobility, as well as many of the most extraordinary Americans, who, as she said, had made everything of her and with whom she had remained, often, in correspondence; while Miss Amy, after all less conventional, at the end of long years of London, abounded in reminiscences of literary, artistic, and even – Miss Susan heard it with bated breath – theatrical society, under the influence of which she had written – there, it came out! – a novel that had been anonymously published and a play that had been strikingly type-copied. Not the least charm, clearly, of this picturesque outlook at Marr would be the support that might be drawn from it for getting back, as she hinted, with "general society" bravely sacrificed, to "real work." She had in her head hundreds of plots – with which the future, accordingly, seemed to bristle for Miss Susan. The latter, on her side, was only waiting for the wind to go down to take up again her sketching. The wind at Marr was often high, as was natural in a little old huddled, red-roofed, historic south-coast town which had once been in a manner mistress, as the cousins reminded each other, of the "Channel," and from which, high and dry on its hilltop though it might be, the sea had not so far receded as not to give, constantly, a taste of temper. Miss Susan came back to English scenery with a small sigh of fondness to which the consciousness of Alps and Apennines only gave more of a quaver; she had picked out her subjects and, with her head on one side and a sense that they were easier abroad, sat sucking her water-colour brush and nervously – perhaps even a little inconsistently – waiting and hesitating. What had happened was that they had, each for herself, rediscovered the country; only Miss Amy, emergent from Bloomsbury lodgings, spoke of it as primroses and sunsets, and Miss Susan, rebounding from the Arno and the Reuss, called it, with a shy, synthetic pride, simply England.

The country was at any rate in the house with them as well as in the little green girdle and in the big blue belt. It was in the objects and relics that they handled together and wondered over, finding in them a ground for much inferred importance and invoked romance, stuffing large stories into very small openings and pulling every faded bell-rope that might jingle rustily into the past. They were still here in the presence, at all events, of their common ancestors, as to whom, more than ever before, they took only the best for granted. Was not the best, for that matter, – the best, that is, of little melancholy, middling, disinherited Marr, – seated in every stiff chair of the decent old house and stitched into the patchwork of every quaint old counterpane? Two hundred years of it squared themselves in the brown, panelled parlour, creaked patiently on the wide staircase, and bloomed herbaceously in the red-walled garden. There was nothing any one had ever done or been at Marr that a Frush hadn't done it or been it. Yet they wanted more of a picture and talked themselves into the fancy of it; there were portraits – half a dozen, comparatively recent (they called 1800 comparatively recent), and something of a trial to a descendant who had copied Titian at the Pitti; but they were curious of detail and would have liked to people a little more thickly their backward space, to set it up behind their chairs as a screen embossed with figures. They threw off theories and small imaginations, and almost conceived themselves engaged in researches; all of which made for pomp and circumstance. Their desire was to discover something, and, emboldened by the broader sweep of wing of her companion, Miss Susan herself was not afraid of discovering something bad. Miss Amy it was who had first remarked, as a warning, that this was what it might all lead to. It was she, moreover, to whom they owed the formula that, had anything *very* bad ever happened at Marr, they should be sorry if a Frush hadn't been in it. This was the moment at which Miss Susan's spirit had reached its highest point: she had declared, with her odd, breathless laugh, a prolonged, an alarmed or alarming gasp, that she should really be quite ashamed. And so they rested awhile; not saying quite how far they were prepared to go in crime – not giving the matter a name. But there would have been little doubt for an observer that each supposed the other to mean that she not only didn't draw the line at murder, but stretched it so as to take in – well, gay deception. If Miss Susan could conceivably have asked whether Don Juan had ever touched at that port, Miss Amy would, to a certainty, have wanted to know by way of answer at what port he had *not* touched. It was only unfortunately true that no one of the portraits of gentlemen looked at all like him and no one of those of ladies suggested one of his victims.

At last, none the less, the cousins had a find, came upon

9

a box of old odds and ends, mainly documentary; partly printed matter, newspapers and pamphlets yellow and grey with time, and, for the rest, epistolary – several packets of letters, faded, scarce decipherable, but clearly sorted for preservation and tied, with sprigged ribbon of a far-away fashion, into little groups. Marr, below ground, is solidly founded – underlaid with great straddling cellars, sound and dry, that are like the groined crypts of churches and that present themselves to the meagre modern conception as the treasure-chambers of stout merchants and bankers in the old bustling days. A recess in the thickness of one of the walls had yielded up, on resolute investigation – that of the local youth employed for odd jobs and who had happened to explore in this direction on his own account – a collection of rusty superfluities among which the small chest in question had been dragged to light. It produced of course an instant impression and figured as a discovery; though indeed as rather a deceptive one on its having, when forced open, nothing better to show, at the best, than a quantity of rather illegible correspondence. The good ladies had naturally had for the moment a fluttered hope of old golden guineas – a miser's hoard; perhaps even of a hatful of those foreign coins of old-fashioned romance, ducats, doubloons, pieces of eight, as are sometimes found to have come to hiding, from over seas, in ancient ports. But they had to accept their disappointment – which they sought to do by making the best of the papers, by agreeing, in other words, to regard them as wonderful. Well, they *were*, doubtless, wonderful; which didn't prevent them, however, from appearing to be, on superficial inspection, also rather a weary labyrinth. Baffling, at any rate, to Miss Susan's unpractised eyes, the little pale-ribboned packets were, for several evenings, round the fire, while she luxuriously dozed, taken in hand by Miss Amy; with the result that on a certain occasion when, toward nine o'clock, Miss Susan woke up, she found her fellow-labourer fast asleep. A slightly irritated confession of ignorance of the Gothic character was the further consequence, and the upshot of this, in turn, was the idea of appeal to Mr Patten. Mr Patten was the vicar and was known to interest himself, as such, in the ancient annals of Marr; in addition to which – and to its being even held a little that his sense of the affairs of the hour was sometimes sacrificed to such inquiries – he was a gentleman with a humour of his own, a flushed face, a bushy eyebrow, and a black wideawake worn sociably askew. "He will tell us," said Amy Frush, "if there's anything in them."

"Yet if it should be," Susan suggested, "anything we mayn't like?"

"Well, that's just what I'm thinking of," returned Miss Amy in her offhand way. "If it's anything we shouldn't know –"

"We've only to tell him not to tell us? Oh, certainly," said mild Miss Susan. She took upon herself even to give him that warning when, on the invitation of our friends, Mr Patten came to tea and to talk things over; Miss Amy sitting by and raising no protest, but distinctly promising herself that, whatever there might be to be known, and however objectionable, she would privately get it out of their initiator. She found herself already hoping that it *would* be something too bad for her cousin – too bad for any one else at all – to know, and that it most properly might remain between them. Mr Patten, at sight of the papers, exclaimed, perhaps a trifle ambiguously, and by no means clerically, "My eye, what a lark!" and retired, after three cups of tea, in an overcoat bulging with his spoil.

II

At ten o'clock that evening the pair separated, as usual on the upper landing, outside their respective doors, for the night; but Miss Amy had hardly set down her candle on her dressing-table before she was startled by an extraordinary sound, which appeared to proceed not only from her companion's room, but from her companion's throat. It was something she would have described, had she ever described it, as between a gurgle and a shriek, and it brought Amy Frush, after an interval of stricken stillness that gave her just time to say to herself "Some one under her bed!" breathlessly and bravely back to the landing. She had not reached it, however, before her neighbour, bursting in, met her and stayed her.

"There's some one in my room!"

They held each other. "But who?"

"A man."

"Under the bed?"

"No – just standing there."

They continued to hold each other, but they rocked. "Standing? Where? How?"

"Why, right in the middle – before my dressing-glass."

Amy's blanched face by this time matched her mate's, but its terror was enhanced by speculation. "To look at himself?"

"No – with his back to it. To look at *me*," poor Susan just audibly breathed. "To keep me off," she quavered. "In strange clothes – of another age; with his head on one side."

Amy wondered. "On one side?"

"Awfully!" the refugee declared while, clinging together, they sounded each other.

This, somehow, for Miss Amy, was the convincing touch; and on it, after a moment, she was capable of the effort of darting back to close her own door. "You'll remain then with me."

"Oh!" Miss Susan wailed with deep assent; quite, as if, had she been a slangy person, she would have ejaculated "Rather!" So they spent the night together; with the assumption thus marked, from the first, both that it would have been vain to confront their visitor as they didn't even pretend to each other that they would have confronted a housebreaker; and that by leaving the place at his mercy nothing worse could happen than had already happened. It was Miss Amy's approaching the door again as with intent ear and after a hush that had represented between them a deep and extraordinary interchange – it was this that put them promptly face to face with the real character of the occurrence. "Ah," Miss Susan, still under her breath, portentously exclaimed, "it isn't any one –!"

"No" – her partner was already able magnificently to take her up. "It isn't any one –"

"Who can really hurt us" – Miss Susan completed her thought. And Miss Amy, as it proved, had been so indescribably prepared that this thought, before morning, had, in the strangest, finest way, made for itself an admirable place with them. The person the elder of our pair had seen in her room was not – well, just simply was not any one in from outside. He was a different thing altogether. Miss Amy had felt it as soon as she heard her friend's cry and become aware of her commotion; as soon, at all events, as she saw Miss Susan's face. That was all – and there it was. There had been something hitherto wanting, they felt, to their small state and importance; it was present now, and they were as handsomely conscious of it as if they had previously missed it. The element in question, then, was a third person in their association, a hovering presence for the dark hours, a figure that with its head very much – too much – on one side, could be trusted to look at them out of unnatural places; yet only, it doubtless might be assumed, to look at them. They had it at last – had what was to be had in an old house where many, too many, things had happened, where the very walls they touched and floors they trod could have told secrets and named names, where every surface was a blurred mirror of life and death, of the endured, the remembered, the forgotten. Yes; the place was h—, but they stopped at sounding the word. And by morning, wonderful to say, they were used to it – had quite lived into it.

Not only this indeed, but they had their prompt theory. There was a connection between the finding of the box in the vault and the appearance in Miss Susan's room. The heavy air of the past had been stirred by the bringing to light of what had so long been hidden. The communication of the papers to Mr Patten had had its effect. They faced each other in the morning at breakfast over the certainty that their queer roused inmate was the sign of the violated secret of these relics. No matter; for the sake of the secret they would put up with his attention; and – this, in them, was most beautiful of all – they must, though he was such an addition to their grandeur, keep him quite to themselves. Other people might hear of what was in the letters, but they should never hear of *him*. They were not afraid that either of the maids should see him – he was not a matter for maids. The question indeed was whether – should he keep it up long – they themselves would find that they could really live with him. Yet perhaps his keeping it up would be just what would make them indifferent. They turned these things over, but spent the next nights together; and on the third day, in the course of their afternoon walk, descried at a distance the vicar, who, as soon as he saw them, waved his arms violently – either as a warning or as a joke – and came more than half-way to meet them. It was in the middle – or what passed for such – of the big, bleak, blank, melancholy square of Marr; a public place, as it were, of such an absurd capacity for a crowd; with the great ivy-mantled choir and stopped transept of the nobly planned church, telling of how many centuries ago it had, for its part, given up growing.

"Why, my dear ladies," cried Mr Patten as he approached, "do you know what, of all things in the world, I seem to make out for you from your funny old letters?" Then as they waited, extremely on their guard now: "Neither more nor less, if you please, than that one of your ancestors in the last century – Mr Cuthbert Frush, it would seem, by name – was hanged."

They never knew afterwards which of the two had first found composure – found even dignity – to respond. "And pray, Mr Patten, for what?"

"Ah, that's just what I don't yet get hold of. But if you don't mind my digging away" – and the vicar's bushy,

jolly brows turned from one of the ladies to the other –
"I think I can run it to earth. They hanged, in those days,
you know," he added as if he had seen something in their
faces, "for almost any trifle!"

"Oh, I hope it wasn't for a trifle!" Miss Susan strangely
tittered.

"Yes, of course one would like that, while he was about
it – well, it had been, as they say," Mr Patten laughed,
"rather for a sheep than for a lamb!"

"Did they hang at that time for a sheep?" Miss Amy
wonderingly asked.

It made their friend laugh again. "The question's whether
he did! But we'll find out. Upon my word, you know, I quite
want to myself. I'm awfully busy, but I think I can promise
you that you shall hear. You *don't* mind?" he insisted.

"I think we could bear *anything*," said Miss Amy.

Miss Susan gazed at her, on this, as for reference
and appeal. "And what is he, after all, at this time of
day, *to* us?"

Her kinswoman, meeting the eyeglass fixedly, spoke with
gravity. "Oh, an ancestor's always an ancestor."

"Well said and well felt, dear lady!" the vicar declared.
"Whatever they may have done –"

"It isn't every one," Miss Amy replied, "that has them to
be ashamed of."

"And we're not ashamed *yet!*" Miss Frush jerked out.

"Let me promise you then that you shan't be. Only, for
I am busy," said Mr Patten, "give me time."

"Ah, but we want the truth!" they cried with high emphasis
as he quitted them. They were much excited now.

He answered by pulling up and turning round as short
as if his professional character had been challenged. "Isn't
it just in the truth – and the truth only – that I deal?"

This they recognized as much as his love of a joke, and
so they were left there together in the pleasant, if slightly
overdone, void of the square, which wore at moments the
air of a conscious demonstration, intended as an appeal,
of the shrinkage of the population of Marr to a solitary

cat. They walked on after a little, but they waited till the vicar was ever so far away before they spoke again; all the more that their doing so must bring them once more to a pause. Then they had a long look. "Hanged!" said Miss Amy – yet almost exultantly.

This was, however, because it was not she who had seen. "That's why his head –" but Miss Susan faltered.

Her companion took it in. "Oh, has such a dreadful twist?"

"It *is* dreadful!" Miss Susan at last dropped, speaking as if she had been present at twenty executions.

There would have been no saying, at any rate, what it didn't evoke from Miss Amy. "It breaks their neck," she contributed after a moment.

Miss Susan looked away. "That's why, I suppose, the head turns so fearfully awry. It's a most peculiar effect."

So peculiar, it might have seemed, that it made them silent afresh. "Well, then, I hope he killed some one!" Miss Amy broke out at last.

Her companion thought. "Wouldn't it depend on whom –?"

"No!" she returned with her characteristic briskness – a briskness that set them again into motion.

That Mr Patten was tremendously busy was evident indeed, as even by the end of the week he had nothing more to impart. The whole thing meanwhile came up again – on the Sunday afternoon; as the younger Miss Frush had been quite confident that, from one day to the other, it must. They went inveterately to evening church, to the close of which supper was postponed; and Miss Susan, on this occasion, ready the first, patiently awaited her mate at the foot of the stairs. Miss Amy at last came down, buttoning a glove, rustling the tail of a frock, and looking, as her kinswoman always thought, conspicuously young and smart. There was no one at Marr, she held, who dressed like her; and Miss Amy, it must be owned, had also settled to this view of Miss Susan, though taking it in a different spirit. Dusk had gathered, but our frugal pair were always tardy lighters, and the grey close of day, in which the elder lady, on a high-backed hall chair, sat with hands patiently folded, had for all cheer the subdued glow – always subdued – of the small fire in the drawing-room, visible through a door that stood open. Into the drawing-room Miss Amy passed in search of the prayer-book she had laid down there after morning church, and from it, after a minute, without this volume, she returned to her companion. There was something in her movement that spoke – spoke for a moment so largely that nothing more was said till, with a quick unanimity, they had got themselves straight out of the house. There, before the door, in the cold, still twilight of the winter's end, while the church bells rang and the windows of the great choir showed across the empty square faintly red, they had it out again. But it was Miss Susan herself, this time, who had to bring it.

"He's there?"

"Before the fire – with his back to it."

"Well, now you see!" Miss Susan exclaimed with elation and as if her friend had hitherto doubted her.

"Yes, I see – and what you mean." Miss Amy was deeply thoughtful.

"About his head?"

"It *is* on one side," Miss Amy went on. "It makes him –" she considered. But she faltered as if still in his presence.

"It makes him awful!" Miss Susan murmured. "The way," she softly moaned, "he looks at you!"

Miss Amy, with a glance, met this recognition. "Yes – doesn't he?" Then her eyes attached themselves to the red windows of the church. "But it means something."

"The Lord knows what it means!" her associate gloomily sighed. Then, after an instant, "Did he move?" Miss Susan asked.

"No – and *I* didn't."

"Oh, I did!" Miss Susan declared, recalling her more precipitous retreat.

"I mean I took my time. I waited."

"To see him fade?"

Miss Amy for a moment said nothing. "He doesn't fade. That's *it*."

"Oh, then you did move!" her relative rejoined.

Again for a little she was silent. "One *has* to. But I don't know what really happened. Of course I came back to you. What I mean is that I took him thoroughly in. He's young," she added.

"But he's *bad*!" said Miss Susan.

"He's handsome!" Miss Amy brought out after a moment. And she showed herself even prepared to continue: "Splendidly."

" 'Splendidly'! – with his neck broken and with that terrible look?"

"It's just the look that makes him so. It's the wonderful eyes. They mean something," Amy Frush brooded.

She spoke with a decision of which Susan presently betrayed the effect. "And what do they mean?"

Her friend had stared again at the glimmering windows of St Thomas of Canterbury. "That it's time we should get to church."

III

The curate that evening did duty alone; but on the morrow the vicar called and, as soon as he got into the room, let them again have it. "He was hanged for smuggling!"

They stood there before him almost cold in their surprise and diffusing an air in which, somehow, this misdemeanour sounded out as the coarsest of all. "*Smuggling?*" Miss Susan disappointedly echoed – as if it presented itself to the first chill of their apprehension that he had, then, only been vulgar.

"Ah, but they hanged for it freely, you know, and I was an idiot for not having taken it, in his case, for granted. If a man swung, hereabouts, it *was* mostly for that. Don't you know it's on that we stand here to-day, such as we are – on the fact of what our bold, bad forefathers were not afraid of? It's in the floors we walk on and under the roofs that cover us. They smuggled so hard that they never had time to do anything else; and if they broke a head not their own it was only in the awkwardness of landing their brandy-kegs. I mean, dear ladies," good Mr Patten wound up, "no disrespect to *your* forefathers when I tell you that – as I've rather been supposing that, like all the rest of us, you were aware – they conveniently lived by it."

Miss Susan wondered – visibly almost doubted. "Gentlefolks?"

"It was the gentlefolks who were the worst."

"They must have been the bravest!" Miss Amy interjected. She had listened to their visitor's free explanation with a rapid return of colour. "And since if they lived by it they also died for it –."

"There's nothing at all to be said against them? I quite agree with you," the vicar laughed, "for all my cloth; and I even go so far as to say, shocking as you may think me, that we owe them, in our shabby little shrunken present, the sense of a bustling background, a sort of undertone of romance. They give us" – he humourously kept it up, verging perilously near, for his cloth, upon positive paradox – "our little handful of legend and our small possibility of ghosts." He paused an instant, with his lighter pulpit manner, but the ladies exchanged no look. They were, in fact, already, with an immense revulsion, carried quite as far away. "Every penny in the place, really, that hasn't been earned by subtler – not nobler – arts in our own virtuous time, and though it's a pity there are not more of "em: every penny in the place was picked up, somehow, by a clever trick, and at the risk of your neck, when the backs of the king's officers were turned. It's shocking, you know, what I'm saying to you, and I wouldn't say it to every one, but I think of some of the shabby old things about us, that represent such pickings, with a sort of sneaking kindness – as of relics of our heroic age. What are we now? We were at any rate devils of fellows then!"

Susan Frush considered it all solemnly, struggling with the spell of this evocation. "But must we forget that they were wicked?"

"Never!" Mr Patten laughed. "Thank you, dear friend, for reminding me. Only I'm worse than they!"

"But would you do it?"

"Murder a coastguard –?" The vicar scratched his head.

"I hope," said Miss Amy rather surprisingly, "you'd defend yourself." And she gave Miss Susan a superior glance. "I would!" she distinctly added.

Her companion anxiously took it up. "Would you defraud the revenue?"

Miss Amy hesitated but a moment; then with a strange laugh, which she covered, however, by turning instantly away, "Yes!" she remarkably declared.

Their visitor, at this, amused and amusing, eagerly seized her arm. "Then may I count on you on the stroke of midnight to help me –?"

"To help you –?"

"To land the last new Tauchnitz."

She met the proposal as one whose fancy had kindled, while her cousin watched them as if they had suddenly improvised a drawing-room charade. "A service of danger?"

"Under the cliff – when you see the lugger stand in!"

"Armed to the teeth?"

"Yes – but invisibly. Your old waterproof –!"

"Mine is new. I'll take Susan's!"

This good lady, however, had her reserves. "Mayn't one of them, all the same – here and there – have been sorry?"

Mr Patten wondered. "For the jobs he muffed?"

"For the wrong – as it *was* wrong – he did."

" 'One' of them?" She had gone too far, for the vicar suddenly looked as if he divined in the question a reference.

They became, however, as promptly unanimous in meeting this danger, as to which Miss Susan in particular showed an inspired presence of mind. "Two of them!" she sweetly smiled. "May not Amy and I –?"

"Vicariously repent?" said Mr Patten. "That depends –
for the true honour of Marr – on how you show it."

"Oh, we *shan't* show it!" Miss Amy cried.

"Ah, then," Mr Patten returned, "though atonements, to
be efficient, are supposed to be public, you may do penance
in secret as much as you please!"

"Well, *I* shall do it," said Susan Frush.

Again, by something in her tone, the vicar's attention
appeared to be caught. "Have you then in view a particular
form –?"

"Of atonement?" She coloured now, glaring rather helplessly, in spite of herself, at her companion. "Oh, if you're
sincere you'll always find one."

Amy came to her assistance. "The way she often treats
me has made her – though there's after all no harm in her –
familiar with remorse. Mayn't we, at any rate," the younger
lady continued, "now have our letters back?" And the vicar
left them with the assurance that they should receive the
bundle on the morrow.

They were indeed so at one as to shrouding their mystery
that no explicit agreement, no exchange of vows, needed
to pass between them; they only settled down, from this
moment, to an unshared possession of their secret, an
economy in the use and, as may even be said, the enjoyment
of it, that was part of their general instinct and habit of
thrift. It had been the disposition, the practice, the necessity
of each to keep, fairly indeed to clutch, everything that, as
they often phrased it, came their way; and this was not
the first time such an influence had determined for them
an affirmation of property in objects to which ridicule,
suspicion, or some other inconvenience might attach. It
was their simple philosophy that one never knew of what
service an odd object might *not* be; and there were days
now on which they felt themselves to have made a better
bargain with their aunt's executors than was witnessed
in those lawpapers which they had at first timorously
regarded as the record of advantages taken of them in
matters of detail. They had got, in short, more than was

vulgarly, more than was even shrewdly supposed – such an indescribable unearned increment as might scarce more be divulged as a dread than as a delight. They drew together, old-maidishly, in a suspicious, invidious grasp of the idea that a dread of their very own – and blissfully not, of course, that of a failure of any essential supply – might, on nearer acquaintance, positively turn to a delight.

Upon some such attempted consideration of it, at all events, they found themselves embarking after their last interview with Mr Patten, and understanding conveyed between them in no redundancy of discussion, no flippant repetitions nor profane recurrences, yet resting on a sense of added margin, of appropriated history, of liberties taken with time and space, that would leave them prepared both for the worst and for the best. The best would be that something that would turn out to their advantage might prove to be hidden about the place; the worst would be that they might find themselves growing to depend only too much on excitement. They found themselves amazingly reconciled, on Mr Patten's information, to the particular character thus fixed on their visitor; they knew by tradition and fiction that even the highwaymen of the same picturesque age were often gallant gentlemen; therefore a smuggler, by such a measure, fairly belonged to the aristocracy of crime. When their packet of documents came back from the vicarage Miss Amy, to whom her associate continued to leave them, took them once more in hand; but with an effect, afresh, of discouragement and languor – a headachy sense of faded ink, of strange spelling and crabbed characters, of allusions she couldn't follow and parts she couldn't match. She placed the tattered papers piously together, wrapping them tenderly in a piece of old figured silken stuff; then, as solemnly as if they had been archives or statues or title-deeds, laid them away in one of the several small cupboards lodged in the thickness of the wainscoted walls. What really most sustained our friends in all ways was their consciousness of having, after all – and so contrariwise to what appeared – a man in the house.

It removed them from that category of the manless in which no lady really lapses till every issue is closed. Their visitor was an issue – at least to the imagination, and they arrived finally, under provocation, at intensities of flutter in which they felt themselves so compromised by his hoverings that they could only consider with relief the fact of nobody's knowing.

The real complication indeed at first was that for some weeks after their talks with Mr Patten the hoverings quite ceased; a circumstance that brought home to them in some degree a sense of indiscretion and indelicacy. They hadn't mentioned him, no; but they had come perilously near it, and they had doubtless, at any rate, too recklessly let in the light on old buried and sheltered things, old sorrows and shames. They roamed about the house themselves at times, fitfully and singly, when each supposed the other out or engaged; they paused and lingered, like soundless apparitions, in corners, doorways, passages, and sometimes suddenly met, in these experiments, with a suppressed start and a mute confession. They talked of him practically never; but each knew how the other thought – all the more that it was (oh yes, unmistakably!) in a manner different from her own. They were together, none the less, in feeling, while, week after week, he failed again to show, as if they had been guilty of blowing, with an effect of sacrilege, on old-gathered silvery ashes. It frankly came out for them that, possessed as they so strangely, yet so ridiculously were, they should be able to settle to nothing till their consciousness was yet again confirmed. Whatever the subject of it might have for them of fear or favour, profit or loss, he had taken the taste from everything else. He had converted *them* into wandering ghosts. At last, one day, with nothing they could afterwards perceive to have determined it, the change came – came, as the previous splash in their stillness had come, by the pale testimony of Miss Susan.

She waited till after breakfast to speak of it – or Miss Amy, rather, waited to hear her; for she showed during the meal the face of controlled commotion that her comrade already knew and that must, with the game loyally played, serve as preface to a disclosure. The younger of the friends really watched the elder, over their tea and toast, as if seeing her for the first time as possibly tortuous, suspecting in her some intention of keeping back what had happened. What had happened was that the image of the hanged man had reappeared in the night; yet only after they had moved together to the drawing-room did Miss Amy learn the facts.

"I was beside the bed – in that low chair; about" – since Miss Amy must know – "to take off my right shoe. I had noticed nothing before, and had had time partly to undress – had got into my wrapper. So, suddenly – as I happened to look – there he was. And there," said Susan Frush, "he stayed."

"But where do you mean?"

"In the high-backed chair, the old flowered chintz 'ear-chair' beside the chimney."

"All night? – and you in your wrapper?" Then as if this image almost challenged her credulity, "Why didn't you go to bed?" Miss Amy inquired.

"With a – a person in the room?" her friend wonderfully asked; adding after an instant as with positive pride: "I never broke the spell!"

"And didn't freeze to death?"

"Yes, almost. To say nothing of not having slept, I can assure you, one wink. I shut my eyes for long stretches, but whenever I opened them he was still there, and I never for a moment lost consciousness."

Miss Amy gave a groan of conscientious sympathy. "So that you're feeling now, of course, half dead."

Her companion turned to the chimney-glass a wan, glazed eye. "I dare say I *am* looking impossible."

Miss Amy, after an instant, found herself still conscientious. "You are." Her own eyes strayed to the glass, lingering there while she lost herself in thought. "Really," she reflected with a certain dryness, "if that's the kind of thing it's to be – !" there would seem, in a word, to be no withstanding it for either. Why, she afterwards asked herself in secret, should the restless spirit of a dead adventurer have addressed itself in its trouble, to such a person as her queer, quaint, inefficient housemate? It was in *her*, she dumbly and somehow sorely argued, that an unappeased soul of the old race should show a confidence. To this conviction she was the more directed by the sense that Susan had, in relation to the preference shown, vain and foolish complacencies. She had her idea of what, in their prodigious predicament, should be, as she called it, "done", and that was a question that Amy from this time began to nurse the small aggression of not so much as discussing with her. She had certainly, poor Miss Frush, a new, an obscure reticence, and since she wouldn't speak first she should have silence to her fill. Miss Amy,however, peopled the silence with conjectural visions of her kinswoman's secret communion. Miss Susan,it was true, showed nothing, on any particular occasion, more than usual; but this was just a part of the very felicity that had begun to harden and uplift her. Days and nights hereupon elapsed without bringing felicity of any order to Amy Frush. If she had no emotions it was, she suspected, because Susan had them all; and – it would have been preposterous had it not been pathetic – she proceeded rapidly to hug the opinion that Susan was selfish and even something of a sneak. Politeness, between them, still reigned, but confidence had flown, and its place was taken by open ceremonies and confessed precautions. Miss Susan looked blank but resigned; which maintained again, unfortunately, her superior air and the presumption of her duplicity. Her manner was of not knowing where her friend's shoe pinched; but it might have been taken by a jaundiced eye for surprise at the challenge of her monopoly. The unexpected resistance of her nerves was indeed a wonder: was that, then, the result, even for a shaky old woman of shocks sufficiently repeated? Miss Amy brooded on the rich inference that, if the first of them didn't prostrate and the rest didn't undermine, one might keep them up as easily as – well, say an unavowed acquaintance or a private commerce of letters. She was startled at the comparison into which she feel – but what was this but an intrigue like another? And fancy Susan carrying one on! That history of the long night hours of the pair in the two chairs kept before her – for it was always present – the extraordinary measure. Was the situation it involved only grotesque – or was it quite grimly grand? It struck her as both; but that was the case with all their situations. Would it be in herself, at any rate, to show such a front? She put herself such questions till she was tired of them. A few good moments of her own would have cleared the air. Luckily they were to come.

IV

It was on a Sunday morning in April, a day brimming over with the turn of the season. She had gone into the garden before church; they cherished alike, with pottering intimacies and opposed theories and a wonderful apparatus of old gloves and trowels and spuds and little botanical cards on sticks, this feature of their establishment, where they could still differ without fear and agree without diplomacy, and which now, with its vernal promise, threw beauty and gloom and light and space, a great good-natured ease, into their wavering scales. She was dressed for church; but when Susan, who had, from a window, seen her wandering, stooping, examining, touching, appeared in the doorway to signify a like readiness, she suddenly felt her intention checked. "Thank you," she said, drawing near; "I think that, though I've dressed, I won't, after all, go. Please, therefore, proceed without me."

Miss Susan fixed her. "You're not well?"

"Not particularly. I shall be better – the morning's so perfect – here."

"Are you really ill?"

"Indisposed; but not enough so, thank you, for you to stay with me."

"Then it has come on but just now?"

"No – I felt not quite fit when I dressed. But it won't do."

"Yet you'll stay out here?"

Miss Amy looked about. "It will depend!"

Her friend paused long enough to have asked what it would depend on, but abruptly, after this contemplation, turned instead and, merely throwing over her shoulder an "At least take care of yourself!" went rustling, in her stiffest Sunday fashion, about her business. Miss Amy, left alone, as she clearly desired to be, lingered awhile in the garden, where the sense of things was somehow made still more delicious by the sweet, vain sounds from the church tower; but by the end of ten minutes she had returned to the house. The sense of things was not delicious there, for what it had at last come to was that, as they thought of each other what they couldn't say, all their contacts were hard and false. The real wrong was in what Susan thought – as to which she was much too proud and too sore to undeceive her. Miss Amy went vaguely to the drawing-room.

They sat, as usual, after church, at their early Sunday dinner, face to face; but little passed between them save that Miss Amy felt better, that the curate had preached, that nobody else had stayed away, and that everybody had asked why Amy had. Amy, hereupon, satisfied everybody by feeling well enough to go in the afternoon; on which occasion, on the other hand – and for reasons even less luminous than those that had operated with her mate in the morning – Miss Susan remained within. Her comrade came back late, having, after church, paid visits; and found her, as daylight faded, seated in the drawing-room, placid and dressed, but without so much as a Sunday book – the place contained whole shelves of such reading – in her hand. She looked so as if a visitor had just left her that Amy put the question: "Has any one called?"

"Dear, no; I've been quite alone."

This again was indirect, and it instantly determined for Miss Amy a conviction – a conviction that, on her also sitting down just as she was and in a silence that prolonged itself, promoted in its turn another determination. The April dusk gathered, and still, without further speech, the companions sat there. But at last Miss Amy said in a tone not quite her commonest: "This morning he came – while you were at church. I suppose it must have been really – though of course I couldn't know it – what I was moved to stay at home for." She spoke now – out of her contentment – as if to oblige with explanations.

But it was strange how Miss Susan met her. "You stay at home for him? *I* don't!" She fairly laughed at the triviality of the idea.

Miss Amy was naturally struck by it and after an instant even nettled. "Then why did you do so this afternoon?"

"Oh, it wasn't for *that!*" Miss Susan lightly quavered. She made her distinction. "I *really* wasn't well."

At this her cousin brought it out. "But he has been with you?"

"My dear child," said Susan, launched unexpectedly even to herself, "he's with me so often that if I put myself out for him – !" But as if at sight of something that showed, through the twilight, in her friend's face, she pulled herself up.

Amy, however, spoke with studied stillness. "You've ceased then to put yourself out? You gave me, you remember, an instance of how you once did!" And she tried, on her side, a laugh.

"Oh yes – that was at first. But I've seen such a lot of him since. Do you mean *you* hadn't?" Susan asked. Then as her companion only sat looking at her: "Has this been really the first time for you – since we last talked?"

Miss Amy for a minute said nothing. "You've actually believed me –"

"To be enjoying on your own account what *I* enjoy? How couldn't I, at the very least," Miss Susan cried – "so grand and strange as you must allow me to say you've struck me?"

Amy hesitated. "I hope I've sometimes struck you as decent!"

But it was a touch that, in her friend's almost amused preoccupation with the simple fact, happily fell short. "You've only been waiting for what didn't come?"

Miss Amy coloured in the dusk. "It came, as I tell you, to-day."

"Better late than never!" And Miss Susan got up.

Amy Frush sat looking. "It's because you thought you had ground for jealousy that *you've* been extraordinary?"

Poor Susan, at this, quite bounced about. "Jealousy?"

It was a tone – never heard from her before – that brought Amy Frush to her feet; so that for a minute, in the unlighted room where, in honour of the spring, there had been no fire and the evening chill had gathered, they stood as enemies. It lasted, fortunately, even long enough to give one of them time suddenly to find it horrible. "But why should we quarrel *now!*" Amy broke out in a different voice.

Susan was not too alienated quickly enough to meet it. "It *is* rather wretched."

"Now when we're equal," Amy went on.

"Yes – I suppose we are." Then, however, as if just to attenuate the admission, Susan had her last lapse from grace. "They say, you know, that when women do quarrel it's usually about a man."

Amy recognized it, but also with a reserve. "Well, then, let there first *be* one!"

"And don't you call *him* –?"

"No!" Amy declared and turned away, while her companion showed her a vain wonder for what she could in that case have expected. Their identity of privilege was thus established, but it is not certain that the air with which she indicated that the subject had better drop didn't press down for an instant her side of the balance. She knew that she knew most about men.

The subject did drop for the time, it being agreed between them that neither should from that hour expect from the other any confession or report. They would treat all occurrences now as not worth mentioning – a course easy to pursue from the moment the suspicion of jealousy had, on each side, been so completely laid to rest. They led their life a month or two on the smooth ground of taking everything for granted; by the end of which time, however, try as they would, they had set up no question that – while they met as a pair of gentlewomen living together only must meet – could successfully pretend to take the place of that of Cuthbert Frush. The spring softened and deepened, reached out its tender arms and scattered its shy graces; the earth broke, the air stirred, with emanations that were as touches and voices of the past; our friends bent their backs in their garden and their noses over its symptoms; they opened their windows to the mildness and tracked it in the lanes and by the hedges; yet the plant of conversation between them markedly failed to renew itself with the rest. It was not indeed that the mildness was not within them as well as without; all asperity, at least, had melted away; they were more than ever pleased with their general acquisition, which, at the winter's end, seemed to give out more of its old secrets, to hum, however faintly with more of its old echoes, to creak, here and there, with the expiring throb of old aches. The deepest sweetness of the spring at Marr was just in its being in this way an attestation of age and rest. The place never seemed to have lived and lingered so long as when kind nature, like a maiden blessing a crone, laid rosy hands on its grizzled head. Then the new season was a light held up to show all the dignity of the years, but also all the wrinkles and scars. The good ladies in whom we are interested changed, at any rate, with the happy days, and it finally came out not only that the invidious note had dropped, but that it had positively turned to music. The whole tone of the time made so for tenderness that it really seemed as if at moments they were sad for each other. They had their grounds at last: each found them in her own consciousness; but it was as if each waited, on the other hand, to be sure she could speak without offence. Fortunately, at last, the tense cord snapped.

The old churchyard at Marr is still liberal; it does its immemorial utmost to people, with names and dates and memories and eulogies, with generations fore-shortened and confounded, the high empty table at which the grand old cripple of the church looks down over the low wall. It serves as an easy thoroughfare, and the stranger finds himself pausing in it with a sense of respect and compassion for the great maimed, ivied shoulders – as the image strikes him – of stone. Miss Susan and Miss Amy were strangers enough still to have sunk down one May morning on the sun-warmed tablet of an ancient tomb and to have remained looking about them in a sort of anxious peace. Their walks were all pointless now, as if they always stopped and turned, for an unconfessed want of interest, before reaching their object. That object presented itself at every start as the same to each; but they had come back too often without having got near it. This morning, strangely, on the return and almost in sight of their door, they were more in presence of it than they had ever been, and they seemed fairly to touch it when Susan said at last, quite in the air and with no traceable reference: "I hope you don't mind, dearest, if I'm awfully sorry for you."

"Oh, I know it," Amy returned – "I've felt it. But what does it do for us?" she asked.

Then Susan saw, with wonder and pity, how little resentment for penetration or patronage she had had to fear and out of what a depth of sentiment similar to her own her companion helplessly spoke. "You're sorry for *me*?"

Amy at first only looked at her with tired eyes, putting out a hand that remained awhile on her arm. "Dear old girl! You might have told me before," she went on as she took everything in; "though, after all, haven't we each really known it?"

"Well," said Susan, "we've waited. We could only wait."

"Then if we've waited together," her friend returned, "that *has* helped us."

"Yes – to keep him in his place. Who would ever believe

in him?" Miss Susan wearily wondered. "If it wasn't for you and for me –"

"Not doubting of each other?" – her companion took her up: "yes, there wouldn't be a creature. It's lucky for us," said Miss Amy, "that we *don't* doubt."

"Oh, if we did we shouldn't be sorry."

"No – except, selfishly, for ourselves. I am, I assure you, for *my*self – it has made me older. But, luckily, at any rate, we trust each other."

"We do," said Miss Susan.

"We do," Miss Amy repeated – they lingered a little on that. "But except making one feel older, what has it done for one?"

"There it is!"

"And though we've kept him in his place," Miss Amy continued, "he has also kept us in ours. We've lived with it," she declared in melancholy justice. "And we wondered at first if we could!" she ironically added. "Well, isn't just what we feel now that we can't any longer?"

"No – it must stop. And I've my idea," said Susan Frush.

"Oh, I assure you I've mine!" her cousin responded.

"Then if you want to act, don't mind me."

"Because you certainly won't *me?* No, I suppose not. Well!" Amy sighed, as if, merely from this, relief had at last come. Her comrade echoed it; they remained side by side; and nothing could have had more oddity than what was assumed alike in what they had said and in what they still kept back. There would have been this at least in their favour for a questioner of their case, that each, charged dejectedly with her own experience, took, on the part of the other, the extraordinary – the ineffable, in fact – all for granted. They never named it again – as indeed it was not easy to name; the whole matter shrouded itself in personal discriminations and privacies; the comparison of notes had become a thing impossible. What was definite was that they had lived into their queer story, passed through it as through an observed, a studied, eclipse of the usual, a period of reclusion, a financial, social or moral crisis, and only desired now to live out of it again. The questioner we have been supposing might even have fancied that each, on her side, had hoped for something from it that she finally perceived it was never to give, which would have been exactly, moreover, the core of her secret and the explanation of her reserve. They, at least, as the business stood, put each other to no test, and, if they were in fact disillusioned and disappointed, came together, after their long blight, solidly on that. It fully appeared between them that they felt a great deal older. When they got up from their sunwarmed slab, however, reminding each other of luncheon, it was with a visible increase of ease and with Miss Susan's hand drawn, for the walk home into Miss Amy's arm. Thus the "idea" of each had continued unspoken and ungrudged. It was as if each wished the other to try her own first; from which it might have been gathered that they alike presented difficulty and even entailed expense. The great questions remained. What then did he mean? What then did he want? Absolution, peace, rest, his final reprieve – merely to say *that* saw them no further on the way than they had already come. What were they at last to do for him? What could they give him that he would take? The ideas they respectively nursed still bore no fruit, and at the end of another month Miss Susan was frankly anxious about Miss Amy. Miss Amy as freely admitted that people *must* have begun to notice strange marks in them and to look for reasons. They were changed – they must change back.

V

Yet it was not till one morning at midsummer, on their meeting for breakfast, that the elder lady fairly attacked the younger's last entrenchment. "Poor, poor Susan!" Miss Amy had said to herself as her cousin came into the room;

and a moment later she brought out, for very. pity, her appeal. "What then *is* yours?"

"My idea?" It was clearly, at last, a vague comfort to Miss Susan to be asked. Yet her answer was desolate. "Oh, it's no use!"

"But how do you know?"

"Why, I tried it – ten days ago, and I thought at first it had answered. But it hasn't."

"He's back again?"

Wan, tired, Miss Susan gave it up. "Back again."

Miss Amy, after one of the long, odd looks that had now become their most frequent form of intercourse, thought it over. "And just the same?"

"Worse."

"Dear!" said Miss Amy, clearly knowing what that meant. "Then what did you do?"

Her friend brought it roundly out. "I made my sacrifice."

Miss Amy, though still more deeply interrogative, hesitated. "But of what?"

"Why, of my little all – or almost."

The "almost" seemed to puzzle Miss Amy, who, moreover, had plainly no clue to the property or attribute so described. "Your 'little all'?"

"Twenty pounds."

"Money?" Miss Amy gasped.

Her tone produced on her companion's part a wonder as great as her own. "What then is it yours to give?"

"My idea? It's not to *give!*" cried Amy Frush.

At the finer pride that broke out in this poor Susan's blankness flushed. "What then is it to do?"

But Miss Amy's bewilderment outlasted her reproach. "Do you mean he takes money?"

"The Chancellor of the Exchequer does – for 'conscience.' "

Her friend's exploit shone larger. "Conscience-money? You sent it to Government?" Then while, as the effect of her surprise, her mate looked too much a fool, Amy melted to kindness. "Why, you secretive old thing!"

Miss Susan presently pulled herself more together. "When your ancestor has robbed the revenue and his spirit walks for remorse –"

"You pay to get rid of him? I see – and it becomes what the vicar called his atonement by deputy. But what if it isn't remorse?" Miss Amy shrewdly asked.

"But it *is* – or it seemed to me so."

"Never to me," said Miss Amy.

Again they searched each other. "Then, evidently, with you he's different."

Miss Amy looked away. "I dare say!"

"So what *is* your idea?"

Miss Amy thought. "I'll tell you only if it works."

"Then, for God's sake, try it!"

Miss Amy, still with averted eyes and now looking easily wise, continued to think. "To try it I shall have to leave you. That's why I've waited so long." Then she fully turned, and with expression: "Can you face three days alone?"

"Oh – 'alone'! I wish I ever were!"

At this her friend, as for very compassion, kissed her; for it seemed really to have come out at last – and welcome! – that poor Susan was the worse beset. "I'll do it! But I must go up to town. Ask me no questions. All I can tell you now is –"

"Well?" Susan appealed while Amy impressively fixed her.

"It's no more remorse than *I'm* a smuggler."

"What is it then?"

"It's bravado."

An "Oh!" more shocked and scared than any that, in the whole business, had yet dropped from her, wound up poor Susan's share in this agreement, appearing as it did to represent for her a somewhat lurid inference. Amy, clearly, had lights of her own. It was by their aid, accordingly, that she immediately prepared for the first separation they had had yet to suffer; of which the consequence, two days later, was that Miss Susan, bowed and anxious, crept singly, on the return from their parting, up the steep hill that leads from the station of Marr and passed ruefully under the ruined town-gate, one of the old defences, that arches over it.

But the full sequel was not for a month – one hot August night when, under the dim stars, they sat together in their little walled garden. Though they had by this time, in general, found again – as women only can find – the secret of easy speech, nothing, for the half-hour, had passed between them: Susan had only sat waiting for her comrade to wake up. Miss Amy had taken of late to interminable dozing – as if with forfeits and arrears to recover; she might have been a convalescent from fever repairing tissue and getting through time. Susan Frush watched her in the warm dimness, and the question between them was fortunately at last so simple that she had freedom to think her pretty in slumber and to fear that she herself, so unguarded, presented an appearance less graceful. She was impatient, for her need had at last come, but she waited, and while she waited she thought. She had already often done so, but the mystery deepened to-night in the story told, as it seemed to her by her companion's frequent relapses. What had been, three weeks before, the effort intense enough to leave behind such a trail of fatigue? The marks, sure enough, had shown in the poor girl that morning of the termination of the arranged absence for which not three days, but ten, without word or sign, were to prove no more than sufficient. It was at an unnatural hour that Amy had turned up, dusty, dishevelled, inscrutable, confessing for the time to nothing more than a long night-journey. Miss Susan prided herself on having played the game and respected, however tormenting, the conditions. She had her conviction that her friend had been out of the country, and she marvelled, thinking of her own old wanderings and her present settled fears, at the spirit with which a person who, whatever she had previously done, had not travelled, could carry off such a flight. The hour had come at last for this person to name her remedy. What determined it was that as Susan Frush sat there, she took home the fact that the remedy was by this time not to be questioned. It had acted as her own had not, and Amy, to all appearance, had only waited for her to admit it. Well, she was ready when Amy woke – woke immediately to meet her eyes and to show, after a moment, in doing so, a vision of what was in her mind. "What *was* it now?" Susan finally said.

"My idea? Is it possible you've not guessed?"

"Oh, you're deeper, much deeper," Susan sighed, "than I."

Amy didn't contradict that – seemed indeed, placidly enough, to take it for truth; but she presently spoke as if the difference, after all, didn't matter now. "Happily for us to-day – isn't it so? – our case is the same. I can speak, at any rate, for myself. He has left me."

"Thank God, then!" Miss Susan devoutly murmured. "For he has left *me*."

"Are you sure?"

"Oh, I think so."

"But how?"

"Well," said Miss Susan after an hesitation, "how are *you*?"

Amy, for a little, matched her pause. "Ah, that's what I can't tell you. I can only answer for it that he's gone."

"Then allow me also to prefer not to explain. The sense of relief has for some reason grown strong in me during the last half-hour. That's such a comfort that it's enough, isn't it?"

"Oh, plenty!" The garden-side of their old house, a window or two dimly lighted, massed itself darkly in the summer night, and, with a common impulse, they gave it, across the little lawn, a long, fond look. Yes, they could be sure. "Plenty!" Amy repeated. "He's gone."

Susan's elder eyes hovered, in the same way, through her elegant glass, at his purified haunt. "He's gone. And how," she insisted, "*did* you do it?"

"Why, you dear goose," – Miss Amy spoke a little strangely, – "I went to Paris."

"To Paris?"

"To see what I could bring back – that I mightn't, that I shouldn't. To do a stroke with!" Miss Amy brought out.

But it left her friend still vague. "A stroke –?"

"To get through the Customs – under their nose."

It was only with this that, for Miss Susan, a pale light dawned. "You wanted to smuggle? *That* was your idea?"

"It was *his*," said Miss Amy. "He wanted no 'conscience-money' spent for him," she now more bravely laughed; "it was quite the other way about – he wanted some bold deed done, of the old wild kind; he wanted some big risk taken. And I took it." She sprang up, rebounding, in her triumph.

Her companion, gasping, gazed at her. "Might they have hanged you too?"

Miss Amy looked up at the dim stars. "If I had defended myself. But luckily it didn't come to that. What I brought in I brought" – she rang out, more and more lucid, now, as she talked – "triumphantly. To appease him – I braved them. I chanced it, at Dover, and they never knew."

"Then you hid it –?"

"About my person."

With the shiver of this Miss Susan got up, and they stood there duskily together. "It was so small?" the elder lady wonderingly murmured.

"It was big enough to have satisfied him," her mate replied with just a shade of sharpness. "I chose it, with much thought, from the forbidden list."

The forbidden list hung a moment in Miss Susan's eyes, suggesting to her, however, but a pale conjecture. "A Tauchnitz?"

Miss Amy communed again with the August stars. "It was the *spirit* of the dead that told."

"A Tauchnitz?" her friend insisted.

Then at last her eyes again dropped, and the Misses Frush moved together to the house. "Well, he's satisfied."

"Yes, and" – Miss Susan mused a little ruefully as they went – "you got at last your week in Paris!"